*For everyone who misses someone —JC*

*To dearest Sunday,*
*and thank you, Zoë —AC*

Cataloging-in-Publication Data has been applied for and may be obtained
from the Library of Congress.

ISBN 978-1-4197-3498-4

Text copyright © 2019 Joseph Coelho
Illustrations copyright © 2019 Allison Colpoys
Book design by Julia Marvel

Printed and bound in China
10 9 8 7 6 5 4 3 2 1

Abrams Books for Young Readers are available at special discounts when purchased in
quantity for premiums and promotions as well as fundraising or educational use.
Special editions can also be created to specification.
For details, contact specialsales@abramsbooks.com or the address below.

**ABRAMS** The Art of Books
195 Broadway, New York, NY 10007
abramsbooks.com

# Grandpa's Stories

*Joseph Coelho*
*& Allison Colpoys*

Abrams Books for Young Readers
New York

It's spring.

I take long walks with my grandpa.
I hold his giant hand.
He says, "You're too old to hold hands."

We explore,

hand in hand,

the budding springtime.

If all the world were springtime,
I would replant my grandpa's birthdays
so that he would never get old.

# It's summer.

Grandpa buys me a racing track.
It's secondhand with missing bits.
We fix what we can together.

We use our hands to
zoom the cars up and down,

up and down,

up, up, up
and fire them off
into deep space.

If all the world were deep space,
I'd orbit my grandpa like the moon,
and our laughs would be shooting stars.

# It's autumn.

My grandpa makes me a notebook
with handmade paper
of brown-and-orange leaves
that rustle when I turn the page,
bound with ruby Indian-leather string.

Grandpa gives me a rainbow pencil.

"Write and draw,

write and draw all
your dreams."

If all the world were dreams,
I would mix my bright Grandpa feelings
and paint them over sad places.

It's winter.

My grandpa tells me tales from when he was a boy,
of Indian sweets and homemade toys.

There are ships,

snakes,

and tigers in his stories.

If all the world were stories,
I could make my grandpa better
just by listening, listening, listening
to every tale he has to tell.

But some tales are silent.

I help Mom and Dad clean
out Grandpa's room.

I find:
dried blue flowers between
book pages, a yellow toy racing car
glued to a piece of track, a length of
ruby Indian-leather string, a ball of
silver foil from every sweet
he ever ate, and an open pack
of rainbow pencils.

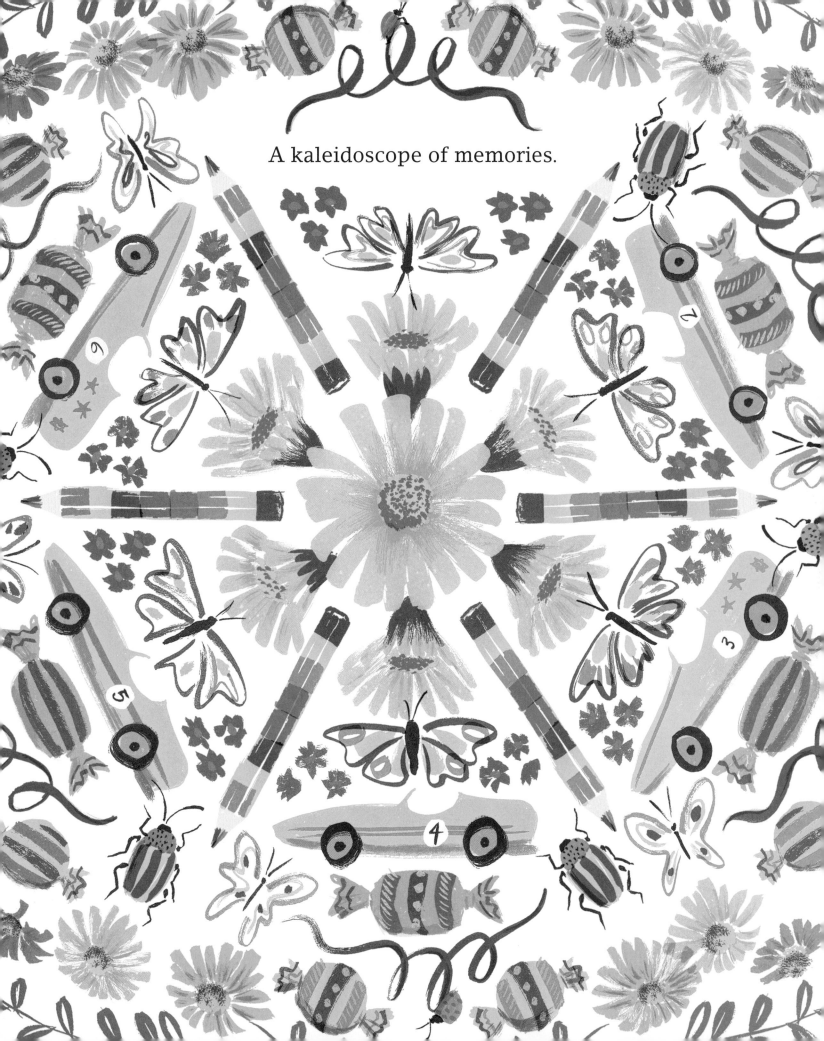

A kaleidoscope of memories.

If all the world were memories,
the past would be rooms I could visit,
and in each room would be my grandpa.

On Grandpa's chair is a new notebook,
newly made with spring-petal paper,
newly bound with a length of Indian-leather string.

My name is written on the front.
It's new and empty
and was made by my grandpa.

So I write
    and draw,

and write and draw,

and write
    all my Grandpa
        memories inside.

I write and draw
lots of different worlds,

and all of them
have my grandpa,

smiling
and laughing,
laughing,
laughing.

He says,
"You're too old to hold hands."

But still I hold his giant hand.
And we explore, hand in hand.